BIG · BOOK · OF FAIRY TALES

Illustrated by David Anstey
Written by Sue Seddon

GALLERY BOOKS
An Imprint of W. H. Smith Publishers Inc.
112 Madison Avenue
New York City 10016

It was a grey and stormy Sunday afternoon. The wind howled through the trees and the rain beat against the windows so hard it made them rattle. It was the kind of weather that ducks love, but dinosaurs hate.

Inside No. 3, Stegosaurus Street, everything was warm and cosy. Grandma leaned forward and put another log on the fire, then she settled herself more comfortably in her big armchair.

"I'm bored!" complained Sammy.

"Me, too!" echoed Crystal.

"It's far too wet for skateboarding," said Grandma firmly, "and it's much too early for tea. How about helping Pops fix the bathroom shelf?"

Pops, Sammy and Crystal groaned. Pops thought quickly. "You know, this is just the sort of afternoon for a story," he said. The firelight cast a big shadow on the wall behind him, and all at once there seemed to be two Pops, not one.

Sammy and Crystal bounced up and down excitedly, and Grandma smiled encouragingly. When Pops told stories they really came to life.

"Are you sitting comfortably?" he asked. His spectacles flashed gold in the light from the fire. "Then I'll begin..."

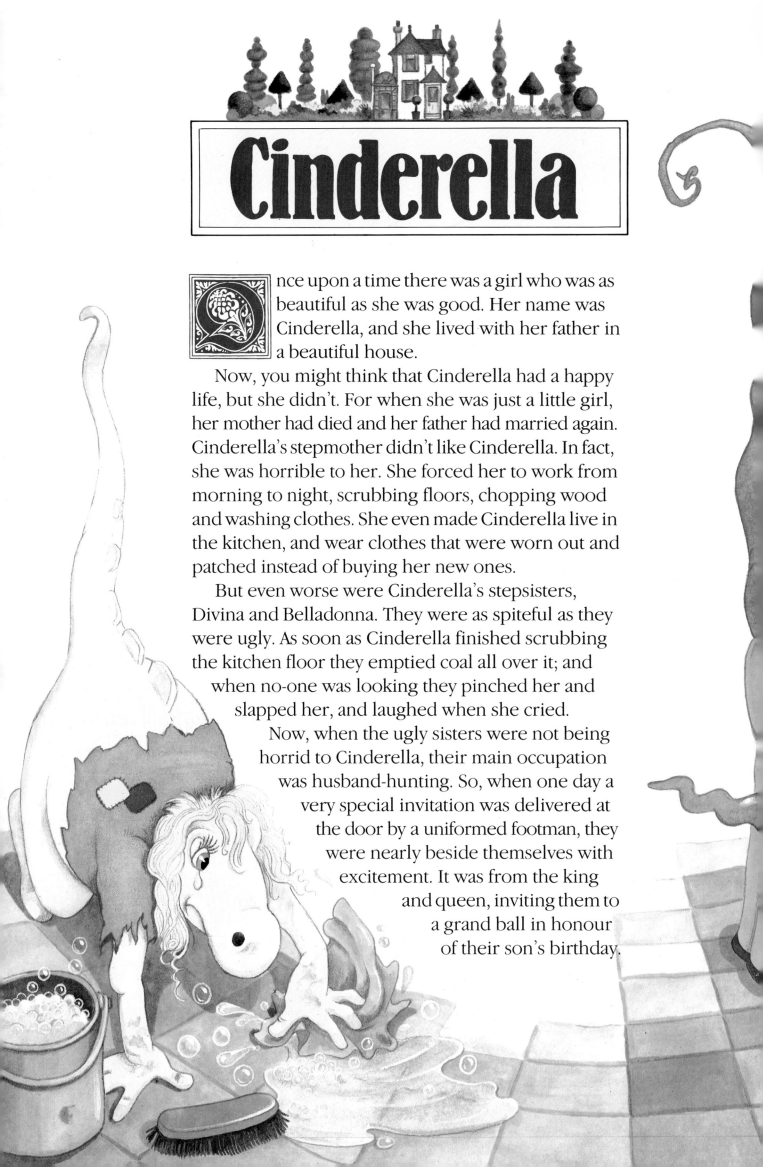

Cinderella

nce upon a time there was a girl who was as beautiful as she was good. Her name was Cinderella, and she lived with her father in a beautiful house.

Now, you might think that Cinderella had a happy life, but she didn't. For when she was just a little girl, her mother had died and her father had married again. Cinderella's stepmother didn't like Cinderella. In fact, she was horrible to her. She forced her to work from morning to night, scrubbing floors, chopping wood and washing clothes. She even made Cinderella live in the kitchen, and wear clothes that were worn out and patched instead of buying her new ones.

But even worse were Cinderella's stepsisters, Divina and Belladonna. They were as spiteful as they were ugly. As soon as Cinderella finished scrubbing the kitchen floor they emptied coal all over it; and when no-one was looking they pinched her and slapped her, and laughed when she cried.

Now, when the ugly sisters were not being horrid to Cinderella, their main occupation was husband-hunting. So, when one day a very special invitation was delivered at the door by a uniformed footman, they were nearly beside themselves with excitement. It was from the king and queen, inviting them to a grand ball in honour of their son's birthday.

"The prince! The prince!" shrieked Divina and fainted to the ground in a heap of pale blue satin.

"Oh dear! What shall I wear?" wailed Belladonna and immediately ordered four new dresses.

Their mother read the invitation, too, and a huge and expectant grin spread across her nasty face.

"A perfect husband for one of my girls," she said. "And a perfect opportunity to catch him!"

At last the great day arrived. Cinderella's sisters came downstairs to show off before they left for the ball. They looked simply awful. All dressed in crimson and mauve, and wearing too much make-up and jewellery, they marched proudly into the kitchen.

"How do we look?" demanded Belladonna.

"You look ...... wonderful," murmured Cinderella. "How I wish I could come with you."

"You! Don't be more stupid than you are already. How on earth could you go to the ball? You don't even have anything to wear," said Divina. And, with that, the two ugly sisters swept off to their coach.

Cinderella sank into her seat by the kitchen fire. She put her head in her hands and wept, repeating over and over again,

"I wish I could go to the ball. I wish, I wish, I wish."

"Then so you shall," said a comforting voice in her ear. Cinderella sat up in astonishment. Beside her stood a cloaked figure with bright, cornflower blue eyes and white hair.

"Who are you?" gasped Cinderella.

"I am your fairy godmother," said the kindly old lady, "and I have the power to make your dreams come true. Do you really want to go to the ball?"

"Oh, yes," said Cinderella.

"Then listen to me," said her godmother. "First, you must go into the garden and bring me a pumpkin."

Cinderella did as she was told and brought back a large pumpkin which her godmother struck with her wand. Immediately, it turned into a magnificent golden coach.

"Now fetch me four mice from the mouse-trap and a rat from the rat-trap."

When Cinderella returned, her godmother touched each animal with her wand. No sooner had she done so than the mice were transformed into four handsome horses, and the rat into a jolly coachman.

"Hmm!" said the fairy. "You can't go without footmen. Find some lizards in the garden for me, my dear. I'm sure they'd enjoy a night out." And, sure enough, at the touch of her wand two large lizards were transformed into elegant footmen.

Finally, the fairy waved her wand over Cinderella. Instantly, her rags became a beautiful pink dress embroidered with pearls; her hair was combed and powdered with diamonds and on her feet she wore delicate glass slippers.

"Now, off you go and have a wonderful time," smiled her godmother. "But remember one thing — this magic only lasts until midnight. You must leave the ball by twelve o'clock or you will be left standing in your rags."

"I promise," said Cinderella and hugged and kissed her fairy godmother. Then she climbed into the coach and rode away to the ball.

At the ball, the prince was bored. He was fed up with husband-hunting girls and their silly mothers. He was just wondering how he could leave without annoying his parents when the chamberlain announced a new guest. The music faded and every head turned towards the door. In the doorway of the ballroom stood the most beautiful girl the prince had ever seen. Cinderella had arrived.

Cinderella and the prince danced together all night. The prince was enchanted — this strange young lady who had appeared out of nowhere was the nicest and most beautiful he had ever met.

They had a lovely time together.

Cinderella also had quite an effect on the young ladies at the ball. They were very put out that the prince danced only with this unknown girl, for each one had hoped the prince would fall in love with her.

"Who on earth is she?" squeaked Divina, who didn't recognise her stepsister at all.

"I don't know," replied Belladonna crossly, "but she's ruined our chances, the little minx."

The prince didn't know who Cinderella was either. He kept meaning to ask her but, just as he was about to speak, the orchestra would strike up another waltz and away they would dance. Cinderella had never been so happy. She forgot all about her miserable life and her horrible sisters. But, most importantly, she forgot about the time, too. So, when the clock began to strike midnight, Cinderella froze to the spot.

"What is it?" cried the prince, worried by the sudden look of terror that spread across her face.

"I'm sorry, I'm sorry," sobbed Cinderella and, with that, she rushed from the room, terrified that her godmother's spell would break before she could escape from the palace.

The prince followed her, but she ran so fast that he could not catch her. He searched everywhere, but she had completely disappeared. Heartbroken, he returned to the palace. On the steps leading from the ballroom he stumbled on something small and delicate — a glass slipper. He picked it up.

"It's hers! I'd know it anywhere," he exclaimed. "Now I shall be able to find her. I shall marry the girl whose foot fits this slipper."

The next day Cinderella was at work as usual, sweeping the kitchen. She had arrived home from the ball in rags, just before her stepmother and sisters. She couldn't help smiling as they went on and on about the splendour of the ball, the handsome prince and the mysterious princess with whom he had danced all night.

"He's obviously in love with her," sniffed Belladonna, "but the silly little fool disappeared at midnight and now he's desperate to find her. He must be mad when he could have had one of us."

At that moment a page from the palace arrived at the door carrying the glass slipper and proclaiming that every young lady in the land was to try it on. Divina and Belladonna went wild. They grabbed the slipper and tried desperately to thrust and push and ram their fat feet into it. But it was useless.

Then Cinderella said, "Let me try," at which her sisters broke into scornful and furious laughter.

"You?" they said in amazement. But the page said it was the prince's order that everyone must try the slipper on. So he bent down and gently slipped the delicate shoe onto Cinderella's foot. It went on so easily that there was an amazed silence.

Then events began to happen very fast — the page ran to fetch the prince who was waiting in his carriage outside, Cinderella's fairy godmother appeared and gave her the matching slipper, and Divina and Belladonna both gave a shriek and sank to the ground, completely overcome.

Cinderella and her handsome prince were married three days later and the celebrations went on for weeks and weeks. Everyone joined in, even Cinderella's stepmother and sisters, and because she was as good as she was beautiful, Cinderella forgave them. And she and the prince loved each other for the rest of their very happy lives.

The Emperor's New Clothes

There was once an Emperor who adored new clothes. He bought them like other people buy sweets. He could, if he wished, change his clothes every hour of every day and still not wear the same outfit again for a year.

The Emperor was not interested in Affairs of State. While his ministers were busy debating important issues in the State Chambers, the Emperor was in his magnificent dressing room, debating whether to wear his suit of cherry-red satin with gold and diamond bows, or the robes of sea-blue velvet embroidered with pearls and coral.

One day, two rogues, called Twist and Smarm, arrived at the palace. They said that they were weavers and they demanded an audience with the Emperor.

"I have, as you know, the largest collection of clothes in the world," the Emperor told them. "What can you offer *me* that is new and exciting?"

"Sire," said Twist and Smarm together, bowing low. "We can weave you the cloth of your dreams. It will be so rare and beautiful that only someone like you, an Emperor of exquisite taste, could possibly wear it."

"Really?" said the Emperor.

"Yes," said the two rascals, bowing even lower. "And that is not all, Your Most Wonderful Majesty. This magnificent cloth can only be seen by the cleverest of people. To anyone who is stupid or unfit for their job, the cloth remains completely invisible."

"What colour will it be?" asked the Emperor.

"Why, Your Most Marvellous Majesty," said Smarm, "the cloth will be the colours of a dragonfly's wing in the moonlight. Threads of gold will glitter through it, like rays of sun shining on the mountains at dawn. And the silver and pearls embroidered upon it will be as splendid as a whole galaxy of stars."

"Truly amazing!" gasped the Emperor. "And can you make a fine suit of it for me to wear on my birthday?"

"Most certainly, Your Most Handsome Highness," said the rogues. "We will start immediately!"

So the Emperor gave Twist and Smarm two thousand gold pieces and a fine room where they could set up their loom, and told them to get to work.

News of the extraordinary cloth spread quickly. Soon, everyone in the kingdom had heard about it and eagerly awaited the Emperor's birthday.

Up in their room, the wicked weavers appeared to work hard. Their candles burned far into the night and the busy clack of their loom could be heard all over the palace. But if anyone had spied on the weavers, they would have seen that Smarm and Twist were only pretending to weave. The loom was empty and, instead of making cloth, the two rascals spent their time playing cards. They hid all the money and the special silk thread that the Emperor had given them in Twist's bag. And whenever they thought of the trick they were playing, they burst into evil laughter.

"What a stupid, vain man he is, to be taken in by us," sniggered Twist.

"And to think that he's an Emperor," gurgled Smarm.

As the days passed, the Emperor longed to find out how the cloth was progressing, but he remembered that it was invisible to anyone who was stupid.

"Suppose I cannot see the cloth?" thought the Emperor anxiously. "How ridiculous I would feel. I will send the Prime Minister to look instead, for she is *very* clever and will certainly be able to see it."

So the Prime Minister went to see the weavers.

"Greetings, Your Honour," chorused the two rogues. "Isn't the material just wonderful?"

The Prime Minister felt a little dizzy, for all she could see was an empty loom. She groped in her handbag for her spectacles and put them on. She dared not admit that she could not see anything. So instead she threw her hands up in amazement.

"Ah, yes," she exclaimed. "Now I see it. How magnificent! What colours! What richness! I will tell the Emperor that the cloth is superb."

As soon as the Prime Minister had gone, Twist and Smarm collapsed with laughter.

"How stupid she was to be tricked so easily!" they cackled. Meanwhile, the Emperor wanted further news of the cloth. So he sent along the Lord Chancellor, his second most trusted minister.

The Lord Chancellor had heard the Prime Minister's description of the cloth, so he was even more shocked to find that he could see nothing at all.

"This must mean that I am not fit to be Lord Chancellor," he thought, miserably. So, like the Prime Minister, the Lord Chancellor decided to pretend. "Your Majesty," he reported back to the Emperor. "The beauty of the cloth will exceed your wildest dreams." And so the Emperor was satisfied that all was well.

At last, it was the day before the Emperor's birthday, and time for the Emperor to see the cloth for himself.

The Emperor and all his courtiers crowded into the weavers' room. The loom was covered with a sheet.

"Your Highness," said Twist, bowing low to hide the grin on his evil face, "are you ready to see our work?"

The Emperor nodded his head and Smarm pulled aside the sheet. There was the loom – quite empty!

The Emperor almost let out a shriek.

"I can't see anything!" he thought, turning quite pink in his panic. "What shall I do? What shall I say?"

Just then, the Prime Minister stepped forward.

"Your Majesty," she said, "look at the richness of the design. Isn't it magnificent?"

"Oh, yes!" exclaimed the Emperor hurriedly. "It is just as wonderful as you said it would be."

All the statesmen and courtiers agreed.

"Excellent! Beautiful!" they cried. But, like the Emperor, they really could see nothing at all. Twist and Smarm picked up the cloth and with great concentration, drew on it the pattern of a suit. Then they pretended to cut the cloth and began to sew it together with needles threaded with imaginary thread. The Emperor and his courtiers watched in amazement. None of them dared admit that the cloth did not exist...

On the morning of his birthday, the Emperor summoned Smarm and Twist to his beautiful, gold-mirrored dressing room. There, under the great crystal and diamond chandeliers, the two rogues held up each piece of suit for the Emperor to admire.

"Here is the coat, Your Magnificence," began Twist. "See how the threads shine in all the colours of the sun at dawn. Yet, amazingly, the cloth is so light, it will feel as if Your Majesty has nothing on."

"Here are the breeches," said Twist. "As you can see, they are cut in the latest style, fastened with jewels and as brilliant as a dragonfly's wing. Now, if Your Majesty will be kind enough to step behind this screen and take off your clothes, we will help you into your new suit."

Behind the screen, the weavers smoothed and patted the imaginary cloth, and pretended to help the Emperor into his splendid new clothes. The courtiers waited, holding their breath and biting their nails in excitement.

At last, the Emperor stepped out from behind the screen and paraded before the mirrors. He looked at himself from every angle, then he turned to face his subjects.

"Well?" he commanded.

You could have heard a weaver's pin drop, the silence was so great. There stood the Emperor, wearing nothing at all!

The Prime Minister was the first to recover.

"You look quite wonderful, Your Highness," she shrieked shakily. "It suits you perfectly!"

"Yes! Yes!" agreed the Emperor. Like the Prime Minister, he was too vain to admit that the cloth was invisible. "It is quite the most unusual suit I have," he continued, enthusiastically. "Give the weavers another thousand gold pieces and let the Royal Birthday Procession begin."

With that, two pages rushed forward to pick up the Emperor's invisible train. The courtiers, all richly dressed in gold, silver, scarlet and purple, formed a long line in the courtyard. And a band of trumpeters struck up a merry tune.

An enormous crowd had gathered along the processional route to wish their Emperor a happy birthday – and to admire his wonderful new clothes. The children had been given a day's holiday from school, and they stood at the front, waving flags. The only eyes that weren't on the palace gates were those of Twist and Smarm, for they were miles away by now – with the Emperor's gold coins jangling in their pockets.

Suddenly, there was a fanfare of trumpets and the Emperor stepped out of the palace. He marched proudly beneath his scarlet and gold velvet canopy, his imaginary train held up by the two pages, and the long line of his ministers and courtiers behind him.

The crowd roared out their approval. Everyone could see that the Emperor's new clothes did not exist, but no one wanted to be thought stupid. So they shouted their compliments all the way along the route. Then, a voice cut through all the noise.

"Look, look! The Emperor's got no clothes on!" It was the voice of a small boy.

"Of course he has!" hissed the child's mother, for she didn't want to be thought stupid. But it so happened that a wise old man was standing next to them.

"Just a moment," he said. "The lad is quite right. Our Emperor has no clothes on at all!" And, all around them, the crowd began to murmur their agreement.

"He's right, you know. Our Emperor is walking down the street with nothing on."

And as soon as the Emperor heard them, he knew his people were right.

"It's true," he thought, in anguish. "Through my own vanity I have allowed those two rogues to trick me. Here I am, walking through the crowds as naked as the day I was born." And the Emperor was just about to run back into the palace when he thought again.

"I have made one mistake. So it is even more important that I do not make another. I shall continue with the procession to show my people that even though I have been tricked into appearing such a fool, I am still brave enough to be their Emperor." So he held his head up even higher, and continued on his way, smiling and waving at all his subjects, especially the children. And all the time he longed to be back at the palace, in the warmth and comfort of his old clothes.

Snow White

nce upon a time there was a beautiful
princess called Snow White. Her mother
had died when she was very small and her
father, the king, had married again. His new
wife was proud, beautiful and very, very vain. She had
a magic mirror hanging on the wall of her room, and
every day, when she was sure no-one was listening,
she would speak to it. This is what she said,

Mirror, mirror on the wall,
Who is the fairest one of all?
And the mirror would reply,
My Lady Queen, let me speak true,
No-one is as fair as you!
The years passed and little Snow White grew up.
She seemed to become more beautiful each day and
everyone in the palace loved her. Then one day Snow
White's stepmother asked her magic mirror,
Mirror, mirror on the wall,
Who is the fairest one of all?
And instead of its usual reply, the mirror said,
My Lady Queen, I tell you true,
Snow White is fairer far
than you.

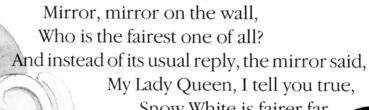

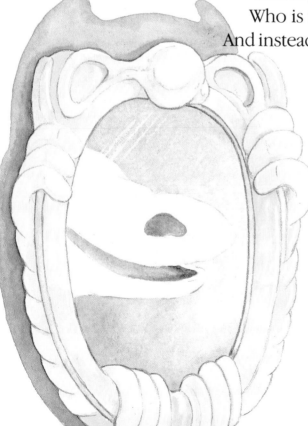

Hearing this, the queen flew into a fantastic rage.

"No-one is more beautiful than me!" she screamed and immediately ordered a huntsman to take Snow White into the forest and kill her.

In the darkest part of the forest, the huntsman stopped and stared miserably at the beautiful princess.

"I cannot harm anyone as lovely as you," he said. "I will let you go, but you must promise never to return to the palace or your wicked stepmother will kill us both."

So Snow White disappeared into the forest. On and on she ran until, at last, she came to a grassy clearing. In the centre of it was a tiny cottage. Snow White knocked at the door. There was no reply so she pushed it open and stepped inside.

Before her there blazed a warm fire, and in front of it Snow White saw a polished table, neatly laid for supper. On it were seven little knives, seven forks, and seven spoons. Upstairs was a large room with seven little wooden beds. Snow White was so tired that she laid down on the first little bed and within minutes was fast asleep.

A short while later, the owners of the cottage came whistling and singing up the grassy garden path. They were seven dwarfs, called Longlegs, Growler, Striker, Digger, Sneezer, Smiler and Nod. And you can imagine their surprise when they found a beautiful princess asleep inside their home!

"Who can she be?" squeaked Longlegs as he looked down at her. But no-one had time to answer him for just then Snow White woke up. She was very surprised to find herself surrounded by seven dwarfs, but they soon made her feel at home.

Soon, Snow White had told them all that had happened and the dwarfs were horrified.

"You must stay here and we will look after you," said Digger kindly. And Snow White gladly agreed.

Far away, on the other side of the
forest, the wicked queen stood in front
of her magic mirror and said,
Mirror, mirror on the wall
Who is the fairest
one of all?

And the magic mirror replied,
        My Lady Queen, although you're fair,
        There's someone else with beauty rare.
        Far away, beyond your call,
        Snow White is the fairest one of all.
At this, the evil queen boiled with fury.
"No-one can be more beautiful than me, I tell you!"
she screamed. "That dreadful child must still be alive
somewhere. I shall seek her out and, when I find her,
she will pay for her beauty – with her life!"
Then the queen ran to her secret room in one of
the palace towers and put some deadly poison into the
rosy half of a delicious apple. Next, she disguised
herself as an old gypsy dressed in rags and set off into
the forest to find Snow White.

At the cottage, the dwarfs were just setting off for work, to dig for gold and jewels in the mountains.

"Goodbye my friends!" said Snow White. "Don't be gone too long!"

"We'll be back soon," said Growler. "Now promise that you won't talk to any strangers while we're away."

"I promise," laughed Snow White, and she waved her friends off down the grassy garden path.

Now, the dwarfs had not been gone for long when there was a knock at the window. Snow White opened the shutters and looked out. There stood an old woman with a basket of rosy apples. It was her wicked stepmother in disguise!

"Hello, my little one!" said the old woman. "Would you like a nice apple to eat?"

"Oh no, thank you," cried Snow White. "My friends the dwarfs have told me never to take presents from strangers."

"Good heavens!" exclaimed the old woman. "What harm could an apple do you? Look, you eat the rosy half and I'll eat the other."

Snow White was feeling very hungry and she longed for a bite of the juicy apple. So, ignoring everything the dwarfs had told her, she took a bite and swallowed. It was poisoned! Instantly, she collapsed and fell to the ground. The evil queen screamed with laughter.

"Well Snow White, your precious dwarfs can't save you now!" And she ran back through the forest to the palace and stood in front of her magic mirror saying,

Mirror, mirror on the wall,
Who is the fairest one of all?

This time the mirror answered,

My Lady Queen, there you stand,
The fairest one in all the land.

"At last, at last!" gloated the evil stepmother, and she kissed the mirror in delight.

When the dwarfs returned home from work that evening, they found Snow White on the floor by the open window. She lay there, quite still, her cheeks as cold as glass.

"She's dead, she's dead!" sobbed Smiler and all the dwarfs wept. Then they put Snow White inside a glass coffin filled with flowers, and left it in the grassy clearing so that everyone could see how beautiful she still was.

Many weeks later a handsome prince came across the glass coffin. As soon as he saw Snow White, he fell instantly in love with her, and vowed they would never be parted. He bent to lift her from her bed of flowers and, as he did so, the piece of apple which had stuck in Snow White's throat flew out, and the poison instantly lost its power.

"Where am I? Who are you?" murmured Snow White, opening her eyes. Then the dwarves came running out of the cottage to see what had happened and turned somersaults in their joy at seeing Snow White alive again

Meanwhile, in the palace, the evil queen stood in front of her magic mirror and said,

Mirror, mirror on the wall,
Who is the fairest one of all?

And the mirror answered,

Snow White is the fairest one of all.
And the rage you feel will be your fall.

Sure enough, in her fury the queen smashed the mirror to pieces on the floor. But in doing so, a splinter of glass pierced her wicked heart and she fell down dead.

So it was that Snow White never again had to worry about her evil stepmother. The prince asked her to marry him and they lived happily ever after in his palace in the mountains. And every summer they went to stay with seven of their greatest friends – Longlegs, Growler, Striker, Digger, Sneezer, Smiler and Nod – in their lovely cottage in the forest.